PHYSICS FABLES

Sarah Allen

Physics Fables © 2024 Sarah McCarthy

All rights reserved.

Cover design by Bookfly designs

Book design by Sue Balcer

Contents

The Tortoise, the Hare, and the Photon:
   A Story of Special Relativity 7

Sakura and the Many-Layered Sea: A Tale of
   Density and Buoyancy 25

Clemmm and the Polar Coordinates 51

The Emperor Butterfly's New Clothes: Exploring
   the Physics of Animal Perception 65

The Wayfarer's Scepter: An Adventure in Magnetism 101

About the Author 119

Also by Sarah Allen

The Fairy Tale Physics Series
    Newton's Laws: A Fairy Tale
    Fluid Mechanics: A Fairy Tale
    Light: A Fairy Tale
    Gravity: A Fairy Tale

Physics Story Games
    The Case of the Seven Reflections: A Fairy Detective Optics Mystery
    The Sorceress of Circuitry: A Steampunk Electricity Adventure

Stick Figure Physics
    Electric Circuits
    Momentum
    Rates of Change
    Work, Energy, and Power
    Basic Fluid Dynamics
    The Complete Stick Figure Physics Tutorials

Math Books
    Practical Percentages
    Algebra 1: Exponents and Operations
    Algebra 1: Foiling and Factoring

About this Book

Hello! Welcome to this collection of short stories about physics!

Each story has some short notes about the physics ideas included, as well as some activities related to the story.

Please feel free to read these stories in whatever way is most fun for you.

My intention in writing this was to create something that you could adapt to your own preferences. Reading the stories without pausing to read the notes—especially the first time through—is totally great and probably the most fun. But I wanted there to be more in-depth explanations and hands-on things to try for those who want them.

Please read what you enjoy and skip the rest. The stories can be read in any order, and there are a wide range of activities and jumping-off points for exploration. Go wherever your curiosity takes you!

If you have any questions or would like to learn more about my project to teach physics through stories, you can email me at SarahAllenPhysics@gmail.com or reach out on my website www.MathwithSarah.com.

The Tortoise, the Hare, and the Photon: A Story of Special Relativity

By Sarah Allen
Illustrated by Vladimir Djekic
Formatted by Sue Balcer

Once upon a time, in a magical kingdom (the gateway to this kingdom is only a quarter mile east of where you live) there was a great race, much like the Tour de France or the Iditarod. In this race, the tortoise was the undefeated champion.

You have probably heard the story. Slow and steady wins the race. The very first time this race was held, it was only the tortoise and the hare who competed, but the next year a cheetah (top speed 70 miles per hour) joined them. The year after that, a thunderclap was admitted (around 767 miles per hour, depending on the humidity).

> ### Science Note:
>
> The thunderclap in this story is the sound of thunder you hear after a lightning strike. Have you heard that you can tell how far away lightning strikes by counting the time between when you see the flash of lightning and when you hear the thunder? It's true! This is because thunder is a sound, which travels much more slowly than light. Light is so fast that it reaches you almost instantly. The sound, though, travels at around 767 miles per hour, which is around 1 mile every 5 seconds. The farther away the lighting was, the longer it takes for the sound to reach your ears. To tell how far away the lightning was, count the seconds between the flash and the thunder and divide by 5. So, 5 seconds is around 1 mile, 10 seconds is 2 miles, etc.

The racecourse was 320 miles long. Year after year, this had proven to be too far for the cheetah, who could only sprint in short bursts. She was determined to defeat the tortoise and solidify her reputation as the fastest land animal, though. (There were other races in which the peregrine falcon dominated, and one in the ocean that the sailfish constantly won, although there was a little clam who was studying hard to learn the tortoise's 'slow and steady' technique.)

No one was quite sure whether the thunderclap was allowed to compete, but they didn't want her to feel left out, so she had been allowed to join. Despite her incredible speed, she hadn't managed to win, or even finish the race, because there

The Tortoise, the Hare, and the Photon

was a thick forest with lots of absorbent moss that blocked her sound waves from reaching the end of the race.

This year, the competition was fierce. Before the race, the animals were warming up, jogging past one another. A horse (55 miles per hour) jogged past a lion (50 miles per hour). The tortoise watched them curiously. She was a bit nervous. Her great great grandmother, the first tortoise, was the one who had first defeated the hare (45 miles per hour). Since then, even as more and more animals joined the race, her great grandmother, grandmother, mother, and even her third uncle on her father's side had all won the race, continuing the family legacy.

This tortoise's name was Eloise, and she had worked hard growing up to make sure she upheld the family name. She had practiced slowly and steadily eating, slowly and steadily walking, and slowly and steadily knitting hats for the family of racoons that lived next door.

Watching all these competitors who were so much faster than her, she began to grow uncertain. Her steadiest speed was only half a mile per hour.

She would just have to do her best, Eloise thought, hoping she wouldn't let her illustrious relatives down.

To distract herself from her worries, Eloise imagined what it would be like to be the lion running next to the horse. The lion was running at her top speed of 50 miles per hour, and the horse was running at her top speed of 55 miles per hour.

"If I were the lion, I would be only a little slower than the horse," Eloise thought. Out of the corner of her eye she saw a grey wolf, trotting comfortably along at 5 miles per hour. "That horse would look just like the wolf to me," Eloise thought.

(This was some very complicated math for a tortoise, but Eloise had always enjoyed thinking about numbers. She had noticed something called 'relative velocity', which is that if you are going 50 miles per hour, and someone goes past you at 55 miles per hour, then compared to you they look like they're going 5 miles per hour.)

She'd noticed this before. When she was stopped, if another tortoise went past at 0.5 miles per hour, that was one thing. But, if Eloise was also trundling along at 0.5 miles per hour, too, she would just comfortably walk alongside the other tortoise. It almost looked like the other tortoise was stopped, as if they were going the same speed.

The Tortoise, the Hare, and the Photon

Eloise's pleasant mathematical musings helped pass the time and soon the race was about to start. Eloise lined up next to the cheetah, the lion, the horse, and the thunderclap, and a tiny mouse raised the starting flag high in the air, lifting a tiny trumpet to her lips.

Eloise took a deep breath, bending her scaly knees and aligning her head with her shell. Suddenly, an animal next to her gasped.

A bright, glowing orb appeared behind them.

"Um, excuse me," the orb said, "Would you mind if I joined your race?"

It was a photon! A particle of light!

The mouse consulted the official rulebook. "Er, well, let me see here. I suppose if there's nothing against the thunderclap joining, then of course we should allow a photon as well. If sound can join us, then light must be able to, as well."

The other animals shifted nervously. Everyone knew that light could travel 186 miles in a single millisecond. (There are a thousand milliseconds in a single second, so she could go 186 miles a thousand times in a single second!)

Eloise knew something the other animals didn't, though. She knew that photons could only travel in a straight line. The racecourse had many twists and turns in it. The photon would never make it to the finish line. She sympathized with the photon, who was so incredibly fast and powerful, but unable to turn. Maybe in the future they could make a new, straight course for photons.

> ### Science Note:
>
> Have you heard of fiber optic cables? These are cables that we send pulses of light through in order to send information from place to place. Kind of like blinking a flashlight to send a message to your friend down the street. The cable allows us to guide the light to where we want it to go, and allows it to turn, which it couldn't do on its own.

At last, the other animals agreed to let the photon join. A few animals quit the race, giving up before it had even started. This was something her grandmother had mentioned. "To win the race you must start," she had told Eloise. "Even if you think it's impossible."

Eloise bobbed her head, nodding to herself as she resumed her crouch at the starting line.

"Oh, thank you so much, so much, so much, for letting me join," the photon said, her voice ringing bright and tinkling like a wind chime.

Eloise smiled warmly, hoping to make her feel welcome.

The mouse dropped the flag, blew the trumpet, and the racers were off!

Eloise's stomach dropped as the other animals sped away from her. The horse and the lion sprinted away, the thunderclap was long gone, and even the hare was quickly out of sight.

Eloise's mother had prepared her for this, too. "When the race starts, you will feel very behind," she'd said. "The other animals will run far ahead, so far you won't be able to even see them. That is okay. Just keep going. Eventually, you will see them again."

For hours and hours, Eloise walked. She listened to the birds twittering encouragement, and the wind twirling through the leaves. Slowly and steadily, she traversed a deep forest, scaled a barren hillside, and squished her way through a wet swamp on the other side.

She was beginning to think that things had changed, that the world was different and 'slow and steady' would no longer work. The other animals were simply too fast.

But then she saw the cheetah, resting on the side of the road.

"Are you all right?" Eloise asked. The cheetah looked out of breath.

"Oh, yes, just resting before my next sprint," she said. "Thank you. Did you see that photon?"

Eloise was happy to chat as she slowly passed the cheetah. "I didn't. It was too fast. It must have been amazing!"

"Yes! Totally amazing!" the cheetah said. "It was going faster than me by 186 miles every millisecond!"

Eloise nodded, not realizing there was something strange about this.

"That is incredible!" Eloise said.

"But the photon didn't make the first turn, so she's off somewhere that way now," the cheetah said, waving a paw. "Anyway, enjoy the rest of your race, you're doing great!"

"Thanks," Eloise said, smiling. "You, too!"

Feeling a little encouraged that she had managed to pass such a speedy animal, Eloise continued.

Next, she came upon the horse, who had paused to eat some grass at the side of the path. Again, they exchanged pleasantries as Eloise passed.

"Did you see that photon?" the horse exclaimed. "She was going faster than me by 186 miles every millisecond!"

Eloise frowned. There truly was something strange about this. "Was the cheetah going slower than usual?" she asked, because the cheetah usually went 70 miles per hour, and the horse went 55 miles per hour. The light should have looked even faster to the horse than the cheetah.

"No, no, the cheetah was a blur, speeding right past!" the horse said through a mouthful of grass.

How strange, Eloise thought. That wasn't how things usually worked at all.

> ### Science Activity:
>
> What is Eloise noticing? For this activity, you need three people. All three people should start in a line, as if at the starting line of a race. Have one person start walking at a very slow, constant speed. Let them get a little ways ahead, and then have the second person start jogging. Let them get a little ways ahead, and then have the third person start running. Keep going at these constant speeds until the runner has passed the other two. Now switch roles. Do this experiment three or four times, until each person has gotten to be the walker, the jogger, and the runner. When you're the walker, how fast does the runner seem like they're going compared to you? When you're the jogger, how fast does the runner seem like they're going compared to you? Notice that the faster you're going, the slower the runner seems to be compared to you.

The strangeness continued all throughout the day. All the animals said that the photon had passed them at 186 miles every millisecond, even though each of them had been going at different speeds at the time. Was the photon speeding up and slowing down to pass the various animals?

Even the thunderclap, which had come to rest in the forest after speeding along at 767 miles per hour, said that the photon had passed her at 186 miles every millisecond.

Impressed with how accurately the animals could judge speeds, Eloise continued, marveling at this mystery.

She spoke with the lion, who said the photon had passed her at around the same time it had passed the horse. Even though the two of them were going at different speeds, they'd each thought the photon was going exactly 186 miles every millisecond faster than them.

"How can this be?" thought Eloise.

But it seemed to be the case. No matter how fast the animals were going, or how many of them were observing the photon at once, each of them thought she was going the same speed compared to them.

The Tortoise, the Hare, and the Photon

    This should not be, thought Eloise. If I'm going 1 mile per hour, and another animal is going 3 miles per hour, then they should seem like they're going 2 miles per hour faster than me. And if another animal next to me is going 3 miles per hour, then the other animal should appear to be stopped compared to them.

    Eloise was so distracted that she almost stopped to think, but this was something her ancestors had all warned her about. "Just keep going," they'd all said.

    So, Eloise kept going.

    For 320 miles, she kept going.

> **Math Connection:**
>
> Math Connection: In the activity above, why did I suggest doing the experiment three or four times? There are only three roles—the walker, the jogger, and the runner—so can you just do the experiment three times? Yes, but does it matter how you swap roles? This is an interesting puzzle!
>
> Can you play around with it and see how to swap people around so that everyone plays every role, and you only run the experiment three times? You could also try solving this puzzle by writing out lists of letters. Call the walker person A, the jogger person B, and the runner person C. Imagine you have three people in a line. ABC would mean the first person is the walker, the second person is the jogger, and the third person is the runner. You could try ACB, BCA, etc. This is something called a "permutation" and there's a whole branch of math that's all about how we rearrange things!

Rounding the final turn, her legs leaden, her heart in her throat, she was just in time to see the grey wolf loping over the finish line.

Eloise froze. Her heart stopped and her limbs went cold. She'd lost.

Her mother, her grandmother, her great grandmother, her great great grandmother, and her third uncle on her father's side had all won this race, each of them facing formidable opponents. She, Eloise, was the first tortoise to ever lose the race.

The Tortoise, the Hare, and the Photon

She felt the stares of the other animals as she swallowed around a hard lump in her throat and walked the last few steps to cross the finish line.

She smiled bravely at the wolf, surrounded by a crowd of cheering spectators.

Her mother and grandmother appeared at her side, patting her shell soothingly.

"You did a wonderful job," her mother said.

"It was a very tough race this year," her grandmother added.

The three of them went out for ice cream.

For several days, Eloise thought back over the race, wondering if there was something she'd done wrong. Should she have walked slower? Steadier? She thought she'd been as slow and as steady as she could.

The mysterious speed of the photon kept coming back to her, too, interrupting her sad thoughts at having lost the race. She wondered where that photon had gone. It must be millions of miles out into space by now, she thought. Far across the galaxy. She wondered what strange and amazing lands that speedy photon was illuminating now.

A few weeks later, Eloise was balancing on her favorite log in her favorite pond, when an idea hit her like a bolt of lightning and she slipped off the log, plopping into the water. It was too strange to possibly be correct.

She scratched her chin and clicked her jaw, going over the facts again. All the animals, no matter how fast they had been going, had thought the photon was going the same speed compared to them. What if this wasn't a mistake?

The implications of this were incredible! A nearby heron chuckled as Eloise clambered back onto her log, thinking hard.

At first, she was so excited that she was thinking rapidly.

"Slow and steady," she muttered to herself, taking a deep breath. She let her thoughts continue at a sedate pace.

"Speed is about distance and time," she muttered to herself. "If my speed if 5 miles per hour, it means I travel 5 miles in a single hour."

The animals had observed the photon to be travelling at the same speed, even if they were going very fast and in the same direction as the photon. The faster they were going, the slower the light should have seemed to them. If speed was the distance travelled in a certain amount of time, then if the speed of light was staying the same then…that must mean that distance and time weren't constant.

Eloise had had several pocket watches over the course of her long life, and they all seemed to indicate that time was constant. But… if light went the same speed no matter how fast you were going, and if two animals travelling different

> **Science Note:**
>
> This is true! Incredibly, strangely, this appears to be the case! This was one of the great revelations made by Einstein. The story goes that he imagined himself riding on a beam of light, and he saw that no matter how fast he was going, light would always appear to be going the same speed. This causes what is known as "time dilation," "mass dilation," and "length contraction." Meaning, as things go really really fast, close to the speed of light, time, mass, and length all change for them. It's a bit complicated how this works, but if you imagine a spaceship travelling really close to the speed of light, things would look normal from their perspective, but if you were on a nearby planet watching the spaceship whiz past, and you looked in through the windows with your telescope, you would see them moving in slow motion. Time would appear to be slowed down. Length gets shorter and mass increases, too. At first this was only a theory, but we now have many observations that show that this is the case, like measurements from clocks in GPS satellites that are going really fast as they orbit the Earth.

speeds could look at the same photon and still see it as going exactly 186 miles every millisecond, why… then that meant that time wasn't measured the same way by all animals. Or distance.

Slowly and steadily, over the course of many, many years, Eloise thought about this idea. She expanded her understanding. She discussed it with an old man with crazy white hair whose name started with the same letter as hers. He agreed with her. Together, they formulated many complex equations about how space and time really worked.

They found that the faster you went, the more time slowed down (as observed by someone else watching you), the more your length contracted, the more your mass increased. And no matter how fast you went, you always measured light to be travelling at 186 miles per millisecond relative to you.

This seemed impossible to both of them, but it led to so many useful inventions and correctly predicted so many phenomena that it had to be true. Eventually, GPS was invented, which wouldn't work without their observations.

Eloise became a very successful tortoise mathematician and physicist. She found that 'slow and steady' applied very well to more than just running races. Her mother and grandmother were incredibly proud of her—as they had been all along, regardless of whether she won the same race they had—and Eloise and all her descendants (who became a variety of things including artists, plumbers, trapeze artists, electricians, and mimes) lived happily ever after.

The End

The Tortoise, the Hare, and the Photon

Science Questions:

Next time you're riding in a car, notice the cars around you.

How fast do they appear to be going?

How fast are you going?

How fast are they going compared to you?

Imagine that there's a car driving in front of you. You speed up and speed up and speed up, but no matter how fast you go, it is still travelling at the same speed compared to you. You can never catch up!

What would this look like to a tortoise sitting at the side of the road?

If you're out walking with some friends, can you ask them to walk at various speeds? Try to be a photon! Pretend your photon-speed is your usual walking pace.

Can you walk in such a way that your speed compared to theirs is always your usual walking pace?

Sakura and the Many-Layered Sea

By Sarah Allen
Illustrated by Donna Schafer
Formatted by Sue Balcer

Once upon a time, on the oily shores of the Many-Layered Sea, there lived a girl named Sakura. You might think that an oily sea sounds worrisome, as if it were the result of a spill or disaster, but this was simply how the sea was. The top-most layer was a quarter-mile thick of oil and plentiful with swarms of oil eels. Which were delicious.

Sakura had short, straight black hair, wore little pink shell earrings, and was fascinated by the sea, as she was fascinated by many things. She had so many questions, but she could barely get them out because she was listening so hard, taking in all the information around her.

One night, she and her grandmother were up late repairing fishing nets. Winds moaned around the corners of their little house, and the drumming of the rain on the roof drowned out all but the loudest cracks and pops from the fire.

"The sea dragon is angry with us today," her grandmother muttered to herself.

Sakura had never seen the dragon who protected the sea, but her grandmother often blamed him when the storms came up.

"Why is the dragon angry with us?" Sakura asked.

"Because we have taken too many of his eels," her grandmother said. "We try to limit how many we take, but this time of year there isn't anything else to eat."

"That doesn't seem fair," Sakura said.

"His duty is to protect the sea creatures," her grandmother said calmly, and for a while they sat in silence, listening to the rain pound like fists against their home.

"Tell me again," Sakura said, struggling with the unruly fibers of the netting. "Who lives below the oil?"

Her grandmother smiled, the firelight flickering off her glasses, but she didn't look up from her work. Sakura marveled as her grandmother's knobby fingers flew deftly across the fibers, untangling and repairing at a blinding pace.

"Below the oil is where the mermaids live, of course."

"And they will grant you wishes?"

"To a lucky few, yes," her grandmother said, twisting two strands of rope together. "Or that was how it used to be. They left in my own grandmother's day. They went to the center of the Many-Layered Sea, where the dragons go to dance, and no one has heard from them since."

"Why did they go?" Sakura asked.

Her grandmother shook her head. "No one knows."

"Then how do you know where they went?"

Her grandmother laughed. "I don't know. That's a good question. Maybe they told us why they left, and we didn't listen. Or maybe they didn't go there after all."

Sakura considered this, then jumped at a crack of thunder overhead.

The next morning, Sakura went out with her father to fish for the oil eels. Rain still poured from the sky in great sheets that sank into the oily waves, descending in great droplets to join the water layer far below. Sakura stared over the side of the boat, her nose close to the shiny surface as the thick waves slowly heaved and ebbed.

No shimmering shadows of eels today. She squinted, trying to make out the water below the oil, straining for a glimpse of a long-nosed mermaid looking back at her, or a flick of tail, but there was nothing. There were other, thicker layers below that, with unnamed armored creatures lumbering through it, she had heard, but she had never seen them either.

Science Note:

The Many-Layered Sea has a layer of oil on top and water below that. Why is the oil on top? Oil floats on water because it is less dense. What is density? Well, if you had two buckets, one full of water and one full of oil, the bucket full of water would be heavier. Because the water is heavier, it ends up below the oil.

Density is the amount of stuff a given size object contains. Imagine taking a slice of cake and squishing it into as small of a ball as possible. You're packing it more tightly, which increases the density!

They caught only a single eel that day, and the next they caught nothing. For the next two months, barely anyone in the village caught anything.

The storms worsened. Great bruised clouds bubbled up, crackling with electricity and sending torrents of rain to be caught by the wind and blown into eyes and faces and open doorways. The whole village huddled together in the great meeting hall.

"We have to stop catching eels," her grandmother said, speaking in front of a crowd of elders. "We will only anger the sea dragon further."

"I haven't had anything to eat in three days," a young man said. "We have to catch something!"

Sakura raised her hand, but no one noticed her.

"We must be patient," an elderly man with a long beard said. "If the dragon sees we are obeying his laws, he will send more eels."

Sakura lifted her hand higher and waved it a bit. The eyes of the elders slid over her, like eels sliding over rocks.

"The sea dragon only cares about sea creatures. He won't take pity on us," the hungry young man said.

"Why don't we ask the mermaids for help?" Sakura cut in, unable to hold back, jumbling her words together until the room filled with a tiny beat of silence.

The silence stretched longer. A few eyebrows lifted. One or two of the elders glanced at Sakura's grandmother.

Sakura frowned. It was a better idea than doing nothing.

"Thank you, Sakura. Why don't you go home and tend the fire for me?" her grandmother said.

Sakura left the villagers arguing behind her, but instead of going home, she went to the rocky shore and stood, squinting against the rain, her hair tossed and tangled behind her by the gale. The waves swelled and crashed against the shore, filled with dark shadows of seaweed, but no eels.

There might not be mermaids out there.

The mermaids might already be gone.

She wrapped her arms around her empty belly, shivering.

If they did nothing, the sea dragon might take pity on them and send them enough eels to live. But maybe the sea dragon had decided he didn't want them eating his eels anymore.

Trying to catch more eels didn't seem like it would work, either.

Lightning stabbed down from the clouds like an angular trident.

She ground her feet into the smooth pebbles of the shore, listening to the crunch. Then she spun around in a whirl of pebbles, making for the docks.

She unlashed her small wooden boat, tossed the rope in, and jumped in after it. Her hands went through their familiar dance as she heaved up the mast and hoisted her coral-pink sail, webbed like the fingers of a gecko.

Thunder rumbled as she crashed through the swelling waves of oil. It splashed over the sides of her boat, and soon her fingers were slippery with it. The rain beaded up on her skin and trickled across it.

"I'm going to find the mermaids," she whispered to herself. But what if there weren't any mermaids, after all?

Sakura piloted her tiny craft up and down the waves for many hours until her stomach heaved along with the waves.

At first, she thought she might be imagining it, but a great rushing sound built and built, like a river heavy with snowmelt cascading over a cliff.

A spiraling whirlpool appeared a few hundred feet from her boat. It whirled faster and faster, and she could see the funnel extending deep into the oil, all the way to the water layer below. At last, in a great spray of water, a fearsome dragon with long whiskers appeared. He bared his golden teeth at her, his eyes flashing like the lightning behind him. Sakura cowered in her tiny boat, crouching behind the mast, and stared up at him wide-eyed. It was the sea dragon himself!

"Go back, Sakura," the sea dragon said, his voice washing over her like powerful waves that could crush her into the sea floor.

She clasped her hands and bowed, attempting to be as mannerly as she knew her grandmother would recommend. "Hello great sea dragon. It is an honor to meet you. I apologize for disturbing you, but my family is hungry, and I have to do something. I know you don't want us to eat your eels, so I am going to ask the mermaids for help in finding something else to eat."

"Your family disobeyed my wishes." The cold winds whirled around him, lifting his many long whiskers. His long scaly body whipped and curled in the wind like a ribbon.

From her respectful bow, Sakura noticed a tiny creature with large, luminous eyes hovering at the sea dragon's shoulder.

"I apologize for my ignorance, oh sea dragon, but . . . who is that?" She pointed.

"That is Clyde," he said in his booming voice.

Clyde waved tentatively.

She waved back, and the sea dragon frowned, his moustache drooping with displeasure.

"He is my assistant." The sea dragon cleared his throat and resumed his threatening expression. "Go back to your family." With a crack of thunder, he disappeared.

Sakura couldn't go back to her family. She already knew the dragon was angry at them. She readjusted her sail and continued on.

The waves rose higher and higher, and she thought she could hear the sea dragon's growl in the whistling wind.

Lightning struck her mast, and her beautiful sail disintegrated into flames. She quickly patted the flames out with a heavy cloth. She knew better than to toss fire into the Many-Layered Sea.

Her sail was destroyed, so she pulled out her oars and rowed.

The air grew colder and colder. Her breath rose in clouds, and the rain turned to swirls of snowflakes like the cherry blossoms that were her namesake.

The cold made the oil thicker and thicker, and rowing became very difficult, but Sakura pressed on.

"Interesting," she thought. "The water freezes before the oil does."

> **Science Note:**
> Different materials freeze at different temperatures. It's why we put salt on roads. Saltwater freezes at a colder temperature than water without salt.

At last, the oil froze solid. Sakura sat for a few minutes, straining against the oars, but finally she stood, stepped out onto the frozen surface, and pried her boat up out of the ice. There was a small, boat-shaped indentation in the oil.

"Interesting," she thought again, despite the cold and her exhaustion. "I wonder what makes the indentation exactly that size." She'd seen boats laden with goods that were lower in the water. She could imagine that the heavier boats would make a larger indentation.

She put her boat on her back like a turtle shell and trudged up the slippery, frozen surface, shivering. At the crest of a wave, she set her boat down and made a sled, sliding down into the next trough, where she picked it up and trudged up the next hill.

Night fell, and she slept in her boat, shaking with cold and listening to the soft flakes of snow collecting around her.

She awoke the next morning in a chilly white drift. The sun glowed out of an empty blue sky.

"At least it's not snowing anymore," she thought.

A sound caught her attention. A wet, slapping sound. Her heart leapt. Was that a mermaid?

She clambered over the side of her boat and flopped into the snow on the other side. It was only an eel, stuck partway in the frozen oil. Her stomach rumbled. She was so hungry. She could imagine what it would taste like, and what being full again would feel like. Her hands shook with hunger as she moved towards it.

She stopped a foot away, watching it flail against the snow.

"No," Sakura thought. "I'm not looking for an eel. I'm looking for mermaids. If we keep eating the eels, we'll only anger the sea dragon further."

But she was so hungry. She'd eaten so many eels in her life. Surely one more wouldn't make too much of a difference.

She bent down, kneeling in the snow with her hands on either side. With frozen fingers, she dug into the solid oil that kept it locked in place.

At last, she gripped the eel carefully and pulled it free, holding it up and examining it.

And then she let it go.

She watched it swish and curl away over the surface. "I'm looking for a new way, not the old way," Sakura thought. But she wasn't sure if she would ever find a new way. That might be her last ever meal sliding away from her.

She sighed and pushed herself up, preparing herself to continue carrying her boat across the treacherous landscape.

Her feet sunk into the oil.

Just a few inches, but it was softer. She took a few steps, her feet sinking further and further each time.

She lunged for her boat, but her feet slipped out from under her.

Half swimming, half crawling through the rapidly thawing oil, she thrashed her way forwards, at last gripping the hull of her boat and hoisting herself up over the side. She slipped and skidded as she landed on the bottom of her boat, which rocked with her movements.

The sea was melting.

She nearly cried as the air warmed around her and the familiar lapping of the sea returned.

A warm rush of fire blasted over the top of her boat, blotting out the sky, and Sakura sat up. The air was filled with dragons, darting and curling. Their jeweled sides sparkled in the sunlight like rubies and amethysts, and they danced and twisted around one another.

For many minutes she sat watching them in wonder. This must be the center of the sea. She had made it at last.

She peered over the side of her boat, down through the clear oil layer, into the watery depths far below. Was she imagining the shapes darting to and fro? She shouted and waved, but the oil was too thick.

How was she going to get their attention? Prying a piece of metal from her boat she dropped it into the oil. It sank rapidly, shooting through the oil layer. When it hit the water layer, it sank more slowly, but it still sank.

"I wonder why it sinks at different speeds in the different layers," Sakura muttered to herself, but she didn't have time to consider this. She had to figure out a way to get the mermaids' attention.

Science Question:

Do you have any guess about why an object would fall more quickly through the oil than through the water?

She looked up briefly, lost in thought, and two inches in front of her face was a tiny little dragon with enormous glowing eyes smiling at her. It waved.

Sakura gasped and pulled back, but quickly recovered herself. "Hello, Clyde!" she said.

"Thank you for not eating me," he said, briefly turning into an eel and back again.

"That was you?"

"Yes, I heard what you said when you were speaking to my bodyguard earlier. I wanted to see if you truly meant it."

"Your bodyguard?" Sakura asked. "You mean, you're the sea dragon?"

Clyde nodded, his large, lamp-like eyes solemn.

"Did you really mean what you said?" he asked. "About finding something else to eat?"

"I did!" Sakura said. "We only want to live, too. And we need to eat something. There's nothing else for us to eat. Only eels live in the oil."

Clyde nodded, still eyeing her thoughtfully. "I will give you the tools you need, but I will warn you, sometimes what we seek can blind us to the true solutions to our difficulties."

Sakura wasn't sure what to make of this, but she nodded and bowed politely. "Thank you, Clyde. I will do my best."

With a sound like a wave breaking over rocks, Clyde disappeared. On the floor of the boat were a single glass bottle, a piece of writing paper, an ink pen, and a pile of sea salt.

In her absolute best handwriting, Sakura carefully printed a message, asking the mermaids if they would speak with her.

She put the note in the bottle, sealed it, and placed it reverently into the sea. It floated. Of course, just like her boat.

"Hmmm . . ." She frowned, thinking. "Maybe I need to weight it down a little."

She uncorked the bottle and poured in a handful of salt.

Recorking it, she placed it again in the oil. It still floated, although this time it was over halfway submerged.

"Hmmm," she thought. "Interesting. Just like my boat, the heavier I make the bottle, the more of an indentation it makes in the liquid."

Sakura and the Many-Layered Sea

> **Science Note:**
>
> Sakura is exactly correct in her observations here. The heavier the boat, the greater the indentation would be. In fact, if you filled that indentation with water, the amount of water you added to the hole would weigh exactly the same as the boat you had just lifted up! This is something called Archimedes' Principle.

She added a little more salt and tried again. The cork barely bobbed above the surface.

Sakura chewed her lip. "If I make it too heavy, won't it just sink all the way to the bottom of the sea?" She imagined the other mysterious layers lurking below.

She only had a single bottle. If she made it too heavy, her message would sink right through the water layer, through whatever other layers there were, and down to rest, lonely on the bottom of the sea.

Chewing her lips and scratching her head, she thought carefully. She remembered the piece of metal she'd dropped. It had moved more slowly in the water than in the oil.

"Why does the sea have many layers?" she wondered aloud. "Why is the water below the oil?" She had never considered this before. It is easy to miss how interesting the world around us really is.

The answer came to her in a flash. The water was heavier than the oil was. That was why it was below the oil. The other layers below the water must be even heavier.

She thought about the indentation her boat made in the oil. If her boat were floating in water, would that indentation be smaller? Somehow, she thought so. The heavier the liquid, the easier it would be to float in it, she thought, although she had no proof.

Was there a way she could test this? She only had one bottle. One chance to call the mermaids for help. She imagined her family and her friends back in her village, hungry and arguing over what to do.

She had an idea. Water from the melting snow still sloshed in the bottom of her boat. She pulled off her boots, which were sturdy and built to be oilproof and waterproof. One she filled with water, the other she filled with oil. She then removed her shell earrings and placed one on the surface of the water, the other on the surface of the oil. They floated there like little shell boats.

She watched them closely, but it was hard to tell if one rested lower in the water. So she weighed them each down with an equal amount of salt. Now it was clear. The shell boat floating on the surface of the oil was riding much lower in the water.

Slowly, one grain at a time, she added salt to each boat. They sank lower and lower, and finally she added one more grain to each boat and the shell on the surface of the oil sank to the bottom of her shoe.

The shell on the surface of the water still floated.

Grinning, her heart pounding, she knew she'd figured it out. If she put just the right amount of salt into the bottle, it would sink through the oil but float on the water below. A mermaid was sure to see it then. She took the bottle with her message, added a few more grains of salt, and replaced the cork. Now it just barely floated. She added one more grain of salt and replaced it in the oil.

> ### Science Activity:
> You can try sending a message to the mermaids, too! Fill a narrow container halfway with water, then pour in some oil (canola oil works) to make a second layer. Next, find a small, sealable container to carry your message. See if you can perfectly weight the container with salt or sand so that when you drop it in, it sinks through the oil but floats on the water.

Her throat clenched as it dropped below the surface of the oil. She watched it going deeper and deeper.

"Please let it stop," she whispered. If she'd added too much salt, it would sink straight through the water and disappear forever, taking her only chance with it.

It hit the water and slowed, then bobbed back up, floating perfectly at the surface between the two liquids. Sakura almost cried with relief, laughing.

Almost immediately, a watery shadow approached.

Unable to look away or even blink, Sakura gripped the slippery sides of her boat, staring at the shadow.

Sarah Allen

The oil began to bubble around her, two waves of oil parted, and she found her whole boat sinking into an indentation in the oil that deepened into a valley and then a large pit. Lower and lower she went until the sky was a single blue circle, like a blue sun overhead surrounded by walls of oil. At last, her boat floated on the surface of . . . water. A strange, more stable feeling than floating on oil, she felt. But she didn't have long to think this, because a mermaid broke the surface and appeared before her, supported by a rising wave of water.

She wore a coral crown and a seaweed tunic. Tiny conch shells adorned her ears and metal rings of various sizes and thicknesses graced her sharp-nailed fingers, which were gripping a barnacle-encrusted trident. Spines sprouted along her shoulders, and when she blinked a second thin film covered her eye briefly from the side, like the double blink of a lizard.

"You dropped this," she said, handing the bottle to Sakura. Her voice was sharp, and it vibrated and undulated like an out of tune violin.

Sakura gasped and shut her mouth, which had been gaping open as she stared at the mermaid.

"Hello," she said. "I'm sorry to bother you, but my family is starving."

The mermaid's gaze travelled over Sakura's arms, clothes, and hair. Sakura couldn't help but notice that the water below was teeming with schools of silver fish, darting and flashing like an enormous, loose-scaled eel.

The mermaid's eyes widened and welled up with tears. "I'm so sorry to hear that! That's terrible!"

Sakura's chest felt lighter. "Thank you so much." She hadn't thought further than this point. How did one ask a mermaid for a wish? "Umm . . . could you help us?"

The mermaid looked at her, blinked a few times. "I'm sorry, what?"

"Er, could you help us?"

The mermaid scratched the side of her head with the tip of her trident. "Um, I mean, what did you have in mind?"

"Don't you . . . don't you grant wishes?" Sakura asked, blushing.

The mermaid's face fell, and the tears spilled down her cheeks.

> ### Science Activity:
> To see density in action, grab a cup or bowl, a scale, some gravel, and some sand. Fill the cup with gravel and place it on the scale. How much does it weigh? Now, leaving the gravel, pour sand into the cup around it. What happens to the weight? By filling in the empty spaces of the cup, you've increased the density! The cup remains the same size, but it's more tightly packed, so it's heavier!

"Oh gosh. I am so, so sorry little split-fin. There was one mermaid who used to pretend she could grant wishes."

What was a split-fin? She looked down at her legs. She supposed one could think of her legs as a fin divided in half. "What do you mean, pretend?" she asked.

The mermaid looked down at her hands sadly. "Oh, she would wave her trident around, tap their heads with it, give them shiny rocks or clumps of kelp. I . . . I think she liked to think she was helping them."

Sakura struggled to wrap her mind around this. That couldn't be true, could it? If mermaids were real, that meant the stories were real! If the mermaids couldn't help, what had been the purpose of her whole journey?

"Please, there must be something you can do," Sakura said, her voice taking on a desperate edge. "Can you send fish up into the oil?"

"They would die there," the mermaid said, looking horror-stricken.

"But, but . . ."

"I'm just a single person like you," the mermaid said. "I don't have power over the fish."

Sakura bit her lip and tried not to cry. She was so hungry. She'd come so far.

"What should I do?" she asked, partly to the mermaid and partly to herself.

"I don't know," the mermaid said. "I'm so so so so sorry." She was crying in earnest now and shaking her head. "Good luck!"

The last of her words became a torrent of bubbles as she sank beneath the waves, and the oil began to refill the hole, lifting Sakura's boat gently up to the surface.

Sakura lay for a long time in the bottom of her boat, staring up into the blue blankness of the sky. She was too weak to move, even if she wanted to. She was alone, with a broken boat, floating in the middle of the sea. She'd gone as far as she could. She'd done what she set out to do, but it hadn't worked out like she'd thought. If even finding the mermaids didn't help, what hope could there possibly be?

Then Clyde appeared.

"I assumed if I told you, you would think it was another trick," he said softly.

Sakura wiped away her tears but didn't move from the bottom of the boat.

"This whole trip was for nothing," she said. Every obstacle she'd overcome, every challenge she'd worked through, she had nothing to show for it.

"No journey is ever wasted," Clyde said.

"I'm hungrier than when I started. My boat is broken. I don't know how to find my way home. I'm no closer to helping my family."

"Sometimes," Clyde said, "we need a reason to take a journey, but we almost always find that what we sought at first wasn't the right thing to be looking for."

Sakura's head lifted an inch and she peered at the cheerful little dragon.

His moustache twirled as he went on. "Would it be irritatingly mysterious if I told you that you've already found everything you need to solve your problem?"

"Yes. Absolutely," Sakura said.

Clyde shrugged. "Well, that's just my nature, I guess. If it helps, here's a scone."

A small yellow lump appeared in her lap.

"What's a scone?" she said, poking at it. But Clyde had disappeared.

After a few more hesitant pokes, her hunger overcame her, and she took a small nibble. Then she crammed half of it into her mouth, chewed, and swallowed.

Scones, it turned out, were even more delicious than eels.

Sakura inhaled every last crumb of the celestial pastry, her delight overwhelming her urge to grumble about Clyde's mysterious advice. But after she'd eaten the entire thing and taken a nap in the sunshine while bobbing gently on the waves, she awoke with a start. As she'd slept, her mind had worked, putting together the pieces of what she'd learned on her journey. The weights of the different layers, the plentiful fish far below the surface. The way things floated or sank depending on how much they weighed and how much space they took up.

> ### Science Question:
> What would you do in Sakura's situation? Do you have any ideas about how she might help feed her village?

"Okay, Clyde, I see what you mean," she said to the clouds. Even though her journey hadn't ended the way she'd expected, she had still found a solution to her troubles. A way to feed her family. She paused. "Still annoying, though!"

Now, how to get home? She rubbed her hands together and picked up her oars.

On her way home, she briefly invented two different ways of navigating. One with the stars, and one with the sun and the currents.

When she arrived at her village, everyone looked about as happy as she'd felt before Clyde had given her the scone. Unfortunately, she didn't have any more scones to distribute.

Her grandmother ran down the rocky beach and helped Sakura pull the boat up the shore. She hauled her out and wrapped her in an enormous hug while berating her for running off alone like that.

When Sakura was finally able to detach herself, she called the rest of the villagers to her. She took one of their eel traps, tied a rope to it, and then lashed it to the perfectly weighted bottle, which the mermaid had given back to her. Then she dropped it off the end of their longest dock.

The villagers all peered over her shoulder in confusion, giving each other worried looks as the trap dropped down through the oil and into the water below, where it bobbed calmly. Sakura waited a few minutes, then hauled it back up. It was absolutely bursting with fish.

The villagers stared at her in disbelief. Moments ago, they'd been ready to give her grandmother their condolences that Sakura had gone mad. First there was silence and confusion, and then cheers erupted.

Sakura was hugged and then hugged again. The villagers lifted her into the air, dancing with her on their shoulders all the way back to the meeting hall where people made short work of cooking up the fish. The feast lasted a full week, with more dancing and singing and rejoicing, and Sakura was asked to demonstrate her invention over and over again. She told her story again and again, and her friends and family laughed and cried in all the right places.

One person suggested that the mermaid really had helped. After all, she'd given Sakura back the bottle. Sakura didn't agree, didn't want to perpetuate the myth that mermaids could grant wishes. On the other hand, if Sakura hadn't believed there was a magical solution to her problem, she might not have looked for a solution at all. She eventually concluded that it was complicated and stopped correcting people.

From then on, the villagers only took a few eels from the sea and instead fished in the deeper layers. Eventually, the layers below the water were explored, too, and even more wonderous creatures and plants were discovered there. The people learned to be better stewards of all the layers, and everyone lived in harmony and abundance.

As for Sakura, she made many more inventions and discovered many interesting things about the world. She also spent many years discovering and then perfecting a recipe for scones. Occasionally, Clyde would visit and give her cryptic advice for his own amusement, which Sakura often decoded and used to her benefit. And they all lived happily ever after.

The End

Clemmm and the Polar Coordinates

By Sarah Allen

Illustrated by Nathan Ranieri Moncao

Formatted by Sue Balcer

Once upon a time, in the early days of the first beehives, there was a little bee named Clemmm (the end of her name sounds like humming).

Clemmm was small and thoughtful, with tiny wings, and she couldn't fly very far. The other bees made fun of her as they buzzed off with their strong wings to gather pollen from far off fields.

She watched them come and go, flying out to secret places only they knew (every bee found his or her own flowers, no one ever shared their secret knowledge.)

One day, it was raining hard, and the other bees were staying inside. Some of them started making fun of Clemmm.

"You're useless," one said.

"Even if you found a flower, you're too weak to carry any pollen back," another said.

With tears in her eyes, Clemmm darted out into the pouring rain, resolved to discover the largest collection of flowers any bee had ever encountered. She was determined to return with more pollen than any other bee had, regardless of the difficulty.

She flew and flew, her wings getting sodden. It got dark, and still she looked. The sun rose and set three times, and still she flew through the forest, looking.

Until on the last day, when she could barely move her wings anymore, she found a huge meadow full of flowers. She couldn't believe what she was seeing. Thousands of flowers, all full of pollen.

She gathered as much as she could carry and quickly found her way back to the hive (even though Clemmm was small, she had always been good at finding her way. She always noticed small details, wherever she went.)

The other bees were shocked when she came back with so much pollen, and even more shocked as she kept going and coming back with even more.

Clemmm and the Polar Coordinates

Clemmm buzzed with pride as she carried back another load of pollen, but she'd flown so much, she was so tired, and as she dumped the next load of pollen, her little wings gave out.

The other bees shook their antenna in annoyance and glared at her.

"Even when you find pollen you are useless," one snapped.

"It's all going to go to waste," another said.

Clemmm looked down sadly, thinking maybe they were right, but then she had an idea.

She stood up and began to do a dance. It was a popular bee dance, which she adapted. She shook from side to side, walking in a figure eight. The eight pointed in the direction of the flowers. She danced for exactly how long it took to reach the flowers, then she stopped.

The other bees looked at her confused, so she explained, then did the dance again. She showed them what direction to fly in, and then mimicked flying for that amount of time. Slowly, they started to get the idea, and some of them took off.

It wasn't long before they returned, laden with pollen. That night the hive had more pollen than it ever had before.

From then on, Clemmm was a hero and an explorer. She would fly out, finding the best fields of flowers, then she would come back and do her dance, showing the others where the flowers were. Soon other bees started doing Clemmm's dance. And, working together, they were able to become the most successful and happy hive in the forest.

Unknowingly, in the great tradition of bee mathematicians, Clemmm had invented polar coordinates, which is simply a way of showing where something is by showing what direction it is in and how far away it is.

Today, bees everywhere use polar coordinates to work together, telling each other where all the best flowers are, all because of Clemmm.

What are Coordinates?

Coordinates are simply a way for us to tell one another where something is. The most common way we do this in math is with a grid. We tell someone how far left or right to go, and then how far up or down to go from there.

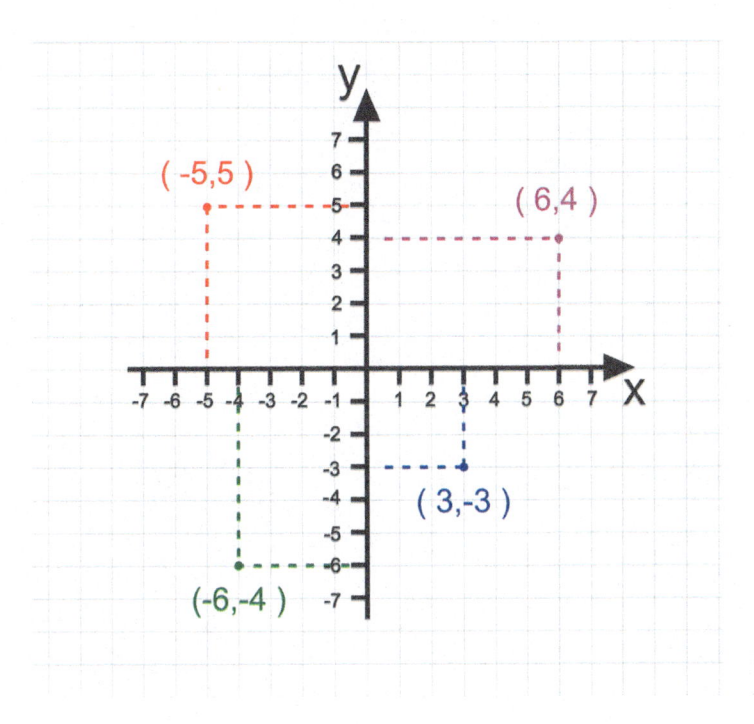

That way of doing things is called the Cartesian coordinate system, named after Rene Descartes (the "I think therefore I am" guy. A lot of mathematicians were also philosophers in the 1600's.)

Bees, however, use what we call "polar coordinates"! They tell each other which direction to go in and how far to go in that direction. Imagine if your friend asked you where your house was, and you pointed in a certain direction and said "Three miles in exactly that direction." That would be using polar coordinates.

Why do we call them "polar"? Because there's an imaginary pole (like the north pole) in the center. All directions are given from that location.

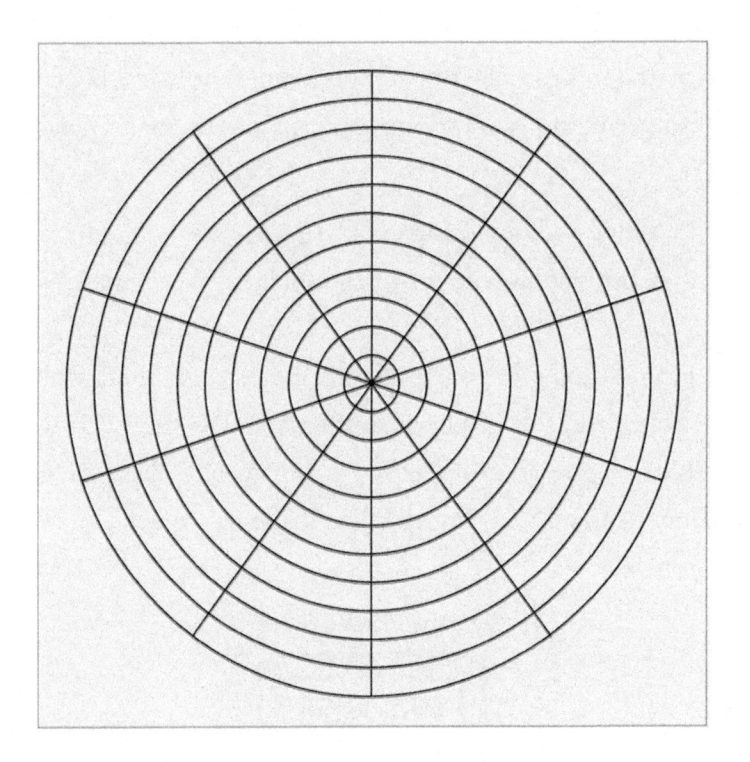

Are they only used by bees?

Nope! We use them, too! They're very useful in physics. Especially for objects that are spinning or moving in a circle. If you try to do the math for objects moving in circles using Cartesian coordinates, you can do it, but the math gets messy and complicated. If you use polar coordinates, it's much simpler.

I love how we can invent different types of math that work best in different situations.

Drawing Flowers with Polar Coordinates

One of the things I like best about polar coordinates is that you can use them to draw loops and spirals and many-petaled flowers.

Let's draw some flowers!

My absolute favorite graphing tool is the free www.Desmos.com.

I'm not going to get into all the math of graphing with polar coordinates in this book, but I wanted to show you what's possible and give you some flowers to play with! Scan the QR code below to a Desmos graph I've made for you.

Desmos Flower Graphs

At the top, you'll see a slider that says "a =". As you select each of the graphs, you can drag the slider back and forth to watch the graph change.

When you first open it, there will be a ton of graphs displayed. I'd recommend turning all of them off except one,

Clemmm and the Polar Coordinates

then turning one of them on at a time. To turn them off, click the colored circles next to the equations.

If you'd like to understand a bit more about the math behind what's happening, read on! If not, skip on to the Polar Coordinates Activity section 🙂

To understand the equations above, we need two quick math definitions.

How do we tell people how far to go?

In math, rather than saying "the distance you should go" we call this the "radius", and we represent it with the letter r. So, if someone told you to go north, and that $r = 5$ feet, they would mean you should go 5 feet.

How do we tell people which direction to go?

Well, the bees probably have the best solution, which is that they dance in a little figure eight that points the direction you should go.

We use something called degrees.

"Science Riddle!

A bear got up and walked a mile south, a mile east, and a mile north...and was back where it started. What color was the bear?

Hint: Try drawing the bear's path on paper. Then, get a globe.

Answer: White! The only way for the bear to have been back where it started is if it started at the North Pole. So, it must be a polar bear."

Try tracing out the bear's path on the globe with your finger. Try some different starting points!

On the picture below, you can see the degrees marked on the circle:

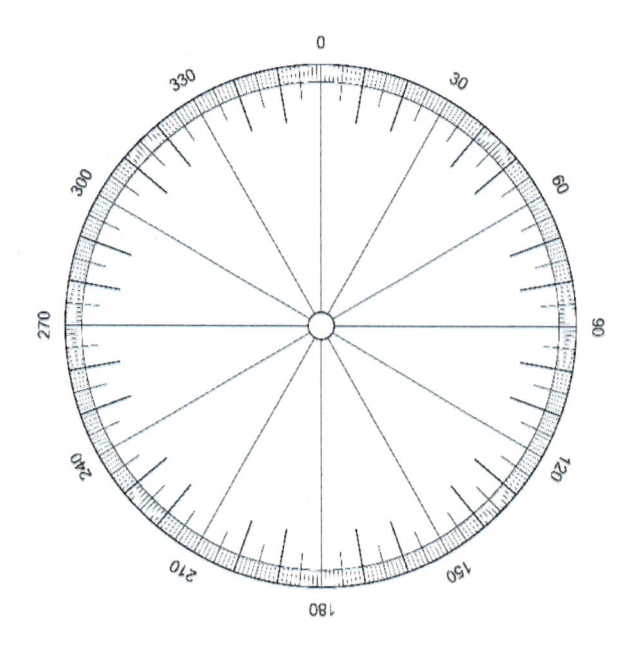

Starting at the pole in the center, if someone told you to go in the 90 degrees direction, you'd go to the right.

(Side note: there are a TON of different ways to write angles, because many people invented their own ways of doing this. Sometimes zero is at the top, sometimes at the right, sometimes they go clockwise, sometimes they go counter-clockwise. In this book, I'll use the circle above.)

Clemmm and the Polar Coordinates

Just like how we used the letter 'r' to represent the distance. We use a fancy Greek symbol to represent the angle. That's the Greek letter theta, which looks like a circle with a line through it.

Polar Coordinates Activity

Materials Needed:

- Protractor
- Post-it Notes
- Pen
- Tape Measure
- Pinecone (optional)

Instructions:

1. Group students into teams of two.

2. Place the protractor on the ground.

3. Put a pinecone on top of it to represent the beehive

4. Draw a few flowers on the undersides of some of the post-its.

5. Shuffle the post-its (some blank, some with flowers) and place them around the protractor, at various distances, with the flowers hidden.

6. One student from each pair now goes and looks under the post-its until they find a flower.

7. This team member must now tell their partner where to look for the flower, using polar coordinates (the angle and the distance).

8. Each flower that is correctly identified the first time is worth one point.

9. Bonus points for using negative angles, negatives distances, angles bigger than 360 degrees, or for doing an actual dance!

The Emperor Butterfly's New Clothes

By Sarah Allen
Illustrated by Donna Schafer
Formatted by Sue Balcer

The sky was an expanse of bright blue and ultra, tilted a quarter-turn to the right. Arnold, an iridescent Blue Emperor butterfly, nervously aligned himself with the angle of the sky as he flapped and fluttered across the ocean waves, dodging plumes of salty spray.

He was late.

Late to the great Conclave, the meeting of all the animals. The last one ever, possibly.

Would any of the other animals even be there? Thirty years ago—many generations back in Arnold's family—there had been a series of natural disasters that had nearly destroyed all life on the planet.

The lion's mother had saved them. She brought the animals together and created the Conclave. After she had passed, her son took over in her stead, and for many decades there was peace.

Arnold flitted nervously across the waves. Should he even be going? Many of his smaller friends—the mouse, the rabbit and the deer in particular—had warned him not to. Many animals were complaining about the Conclave. The predators, especially, were arguing that the danger had passed, and the Conclave was no longer useful.

A great many of those against the Conclave were animals who would happily eat Arnold.

But this might be the last Conclave ever. And Arnold had never been. He wanted to see what it was like. All those animals, big and small, in the same place, working together. Amazing!

The sun sank to meet its reflection in the ocean, the patterns overhead wheeling and tilting with it. Its light reflected in gold and orange shards, brightly horizontal across the surface of the ocean.

> ### Science Note:
> You may have noticed that Arnold sees the world differently than we do! What is 'Ultra?' What does it mean for the sky to be tilted?
> 'Ultra' is ultraviolet light, and the tilted sky is polarized light, both of which Arnold can perceive and we can't!
> For more on both, read the science section at the end.

At last, the island appeared in the distance.

Animals were there, all right!

An enormous, open-air cathedral crouched on the rocky shores of a bay. The clear green water was packed with colorful fish, an octopus, a narwhal, rows of crustaceans, crabs edging sideways through the crowd kicking up sand, a group of dolphins, and a malevolent shark.

Inside the cathedral itself, the space was packed. A bear sat next to an alpaca. Rows of parrots perched on strings overhead like Christmas lights. Crows and racoons chatted and exchanged trinkets.

There was extra space around the fiercest predators: the panthers, the housecats, the eagles and falcons.

They all turned to stare as Arnold fluttered in, blushing and trying to be as inconspicuous as possible. The animals in front gave him annoyed glances, but the animals behind him outright stared. Why was it that so many animals acted as if when they were behind him, he couldn't see them? At least bees and other insects were usually polite. And goats, he'd noticed.

> **Science Note:**
> Butterflies can see almost all the way around themselves, as can goats!

A few whispers ran through the crowd as the lion appeared at the podium.

"He's going to end the Conclave, isn't he?" the raccoon whispered to the crow.

"It'ssss about time," the snake hissed, overhearing them.

The raccoon wrung her hands and darted an annoyed look at the snake.

"Thank you all for coming, my esteemed colleagues," the lion said, his voice echoing off the high, arched ceiling. His mane was streaked with gray, and a tiny pair of gold spectacles perched on his snout.

"I know that many of you," he went on, glancing up at them over his spectacles, "have suggested that we no longer have need of a Conclave."

Some murmurs of agreement came from those with the largest teeth.

"However, I respectfully say that this is incorrect." He paused for dramatic affect. "It is not what my mother would have wanted. Not what she knew was best for all of us." Voices rose, but an ominous rumbling issued from the lion's throat, and the crowd quieted. Arnold shivered. This was exactly as dramatic as he'd hoped.

"Which is why today," the lion said softly, "I will appoint a new king."

A thrill went through the crowd. Heads straightened, beaks snapped shut, and a snake quietly climbed an antelope and rested in its horns to get a better view.

Arnold tucked his wings in nervously, grateful that no one was staring at him anymore.

"Who do you think it'll beeee?" hummed the bumblebee to her neighbor, the hippo. Arnold watched her wings make lazy circles, holding her aloft.

"Oh, it's the grizzly bear for sure," the hippo said, shooting a nervous glance at the shaggy animal resting its enormous paws on its knees.

"Hmmmm . . ." the bee thought. "The shark, though. So many teeth. It's beeeen a while since we had an ocean creature."

The hippo nodded, giving a wide-mouthed yawn. "Yeah, no for sure."

In the bay behind them, crowded amongst the other ocean-living animals and poking its head above the waves, the shark grinned, showing many layers of pointed teeth, her black eyes absorbing all light and reflecting none.

"I have given my decision quite a lot of thought, as I am sure you can imagine."

A few nods here and there. A few glances towards the Great Blue Heron, another favorite for the position.

"I appreciate you all making the time to come this evening. I know many of you have travelled long distances." The lion's gaze fell on Arnold. The warm yellow irises seemed to bore into him, and Arnold crouched lower, bending his delicate knees. Mercifully, the lion looked away. Arnold's antennae shook.

"There are many strong and noble animals that would make excellent kings," the lion went on. "I would like for you to know that I strongly considered the shark." The shark's manic grin disappeared, and her murderous dark eyes sank in disappointment. "I also considered the bear, the falcon, and the giraffe."

A surprised muttering broke out among the crowd. If it wasn't any of these, who could it be? More animals glanced towards the heron. It must be the heron.

"I was deeply inclined towards the heron, as I am sure you can all imagine." The lion swallowed, his powerful throat bobbing. "However, I have made a different choice altogether. A perhaps surprising choice, but one that I feel quite confident in."

The lion rustled his notes. When he looked up, his eyes again fell on Arnold.

Arnold's tiny butterfly stomach went cold. *Surely not*, Arnold thought. The lion wasn't going to pick *him*.

"I have chosen Arnold, the noble Emperor Butterfly," the lion said, the corners of his eyes crinkling warmly at Arnold.

The whole crowd turned to stare. The many-faceted eyes of bees and spiders locked on him. The antelope cocked her head to the side, dislodging the snake as she peered at him. The shark bared her teeth in an angry frown.

The floor tasted bitter under his bare feet. Arnold didn't move so much as a single antenna. He had a strange, wild hope that if he didn't move, no one would see him. Their eyes would simply pass over him, and they would all forget this had happened. King? He couldn't be king. He was a tiny little butterfly. Who would listen to him?

The crowd seemed to agree.

"He doesn't even have any teeth!" grumbled the bear.

"His wings are awfully tiny," the heron said, peering down his beak at Arnold.

The shark simply glared murderously.

The crowd began to close in on Arnold.

A team of security badgers surrounded him, and Arnold let them steer him through the crowd to a tiny door at the side that he hadn't noticed before.

Arnold nervously rubbed his feet together, opening and shutting his wings a few times. The light was dim, and he could barely make out the room around him. The badgers were indistinct shapes, and he had a vague sense of walls and maybe something else behind him, but it wasn't moving, and he couldn't tell what color anything was.

The scent of the badgers was overpowering. Earthy. Like potatoes.

> **Science Note:**
>
> Arnold can't see very well in the dark, but he has a good sense of smell! And taste buds on his feet! (For tasting flowers he lands on.)

"There must be a mistake," he said to one of the indistinct shapes. It was moving, and he assumed it was one of the badgers.

The door clicked shut, cutting off the protestations of the crowd.

"Sorry, bud. The king was quite clear," the shape said. Part of it was swinging, maybe those were arms. "You can turn down the position, though. If you want."

"Yes, please."

"Well, sure, if that's what you want," a disembodied voice from somewhere behind him said. It smelt like another badger, but he couldn't see it. Arnold trembled. He hated darkness.

"It'll likely end the Conclave, though," the badger said.

Arnold's wings stilled. End the Conclave? He wouldn't be alive if it weren't for the animals who had banded together to save one another. But so many of the more fearsome animals didn't want the Conclave to exist anymore. How was Arnold supposed to change their minds? He had no fangs, no powerful jaws or claws. He couldn't sprint or hunt.

He twitched his antennae. One of the badgers had eaten recently, and the sweet scent of honey permeated the room, mixing with the heavy potato smell. Arnold resisted the urge to pat the source of the scent with his forelegs. "Did the king say why he picked me?" Arnold asked softly.

"'Fraid not. Just that it was important."

"Could I . . . speak with him?"

"At the coronation, yeah. Word's gotten out already about his decision, and he had to rush off to stop some rebellions."

Arnold looked down, his antennae drooping. He could never just rush off and stop a rebellion. He wished he hadn't been chosen. Was there really something about him that could help the animal kingdom and save the Conclave? Something that not even the lion could do? His tiny chest fluttered.

What could it be? he wondered. What was different about him?

He opened and closed his wings. He opened and closed them again.

His wings.

One thing he knew to be true about himself, if anything, was that he was colorful. There were so many animals in muted shades of brown or gray, but he was bright and beautiful. Did the lion need a beautiful king? Beauty could be reassuring. Inspiring. Color could be energizing. Lions were beautiful, too, though. In an intimidating way. He rubbed his feet together. The dim shapes of the badgers shifted around him.

He still wasn't sure why this was needed, but . . . the lion was still his king. And the king, by choosing him as his successor, was making a request of him. The lion must know something he didn't. And if that was what the kingdom needed, well, Arnold would do his best.

"All right," he said. "I'll do it."

"Great," the shape said. "The king will be pleased."

"Could I make a small request?" Arnold asked.

"Of course, your future highness." The shape moved in a slight bow.

"Could you bring me the best tailor in all the kingdom?" He paused. "If it's not too much trouble."

✱

The greatest tailor in the kingdom was summoned with all haste, and the next morning Arnold perched on a high balcony of the castle, overlooking the ocean and awaiting her arrival. Warm sunlight bathed the balcony of opalescent shells, and the air was full of currents of delicious scents.

Only a quarter of a mile away a stand of food bushes tantalized him, and he longed to seek them out, but Arnold waited. There was only a day until the coronation, and he had to be ready.

The cold metallic smell of blood jolted him out of his reverie. The team of security badgers surrounding him didn't seem to notice. They leaned against the railings, chatting and idly scanning the castle grounds, but Arnold knew something dark and dangerous approached.

The door to the balcony swung open, and another badger stepped out, bringing with her a cloud of death and peril.

Run, Arnold thought. *Fly. Get out of here.*

But the badgers were there to protect him. He was the new king. There couldn't be danger. Could there?

The first long, hairy leg appeared behind the badger. Then another and another, and Arnold's instincts screamed at him to run.

Eight large reflective orbs, a pair in front and three smaller pairs wrapping around the outer portion of the face, just above the mandibles, followed the legs, and terror shot through him.

Before he could run, the spider jumped straight for him.

She landed so close that Arnold saw himself reflected in her eight eyes.

"Oh my gosh, a king! A butterfly! Let me tell you, people are tal-king!" the spider said. "I'm Sheila by the way, very nice to meet you." She glanced at the badgers and leaned in close. "This floor tastes terrible, don't you think? I don't know how they stand it."

Was this what death was like? Had he been eaten? Was this a dream?

No, he realized. This was the tailor.

"Er, yes," he stammered. "The floor is a tad bitter."

She nodded, hopped left and right, then back and forward a few times, her tiny eyes sparkling up at him.

"I just can't tell you; I am so happy to have an insect king. Someone to represent us." Her eyes shone. "This is exactly what we need, to keep the Conclave from ending."

Arnold shifted nervously, not at all sure he shared Sheila's optimism. Maybe the lion should have chosen someone fierce, like a spider.

"Okay, so what are we thinking?" Sheila lifted her forelegs, holding them up and waving them as if measuring him. "Silk, right? Absolutely silk."

"I was thinking something bright. Something colorful."

"Oo yes, what's your favorite color?"

"Oh, um, ultra?"

"Ooo yes me too!" Sheila grinned again and wiggled her mandibles.

The security badgers glanced at one another, furrowing their brows.

> **Science Question:**
>
> Why do you think the badgers might be confused about Arnold and Sheila's favorite color?

"Er . . . you sure it's clothes that'll help?" one of them said.

Arnold nodded, trying to fake a confidence he didn't feel, but Sheila seemed more on his side.

"Oh, yes, absolutely. When you look good you feel good!" Sheila said, holding up her arms and measuring Arnold.

The badgers exchanged glances and shrugged.

Sheila took a large silk bag from one of the badgers, and from it she started pulling yet more silk bags in all shapes and colors. From these she pulled swatches of fabric, which she held up against his wings.

The Emperor Butterfly's New Clothes

"You're already very colorful," she mused. "And . . . anything I make is going to be tiny. At least in comparison to those gargantuan animals, you know?" She frowned, tilting her head. "I have an idea. Something experimental. Are you interested?"

This was the most skilled tailor in the kingdom, and Arnold needed to make an impression on people, so he nodded.

She pulled a large silk net from her bag, which clanked, and from it she drew large thin sheets of something hard.

"Those are clear," one of the badgers said.

"Yes, yes," Sheila muttered.

"He can't wear clear clothes, can he? It'll be like he has no clothes on at all!"

"Oh, clear things can be colorful," Arnold said.

The badger's frown deepened.

"You layer them," Arnold tried to clarify. Some of his own scales already worked this way. "It's like . . . like the patterns on soap bubbles?"

"Or how oil on water looks shiny and colorful!" Sheila added brightly. "Very thin layers of clear things reflect colors."

"Ah. Sure." The badger gave them a slow nod, as if humoring people who had lost their minds.

Sheila quickly set to work layering scales, crafting a thick, solid cloak that swooped over Arnold's shoulders, with a stiff collar rising dramatically over his head.

For hours and hours, they worked, trying different combinations of scales and examining how the light reflected and refracted through them.

Eventually, as the sun was going down, Sheila hopped backwards, lifting her forelegs and staring at him with eight critical eyes.

"Fabulous," she proclaimed.

The badgers held up a mirror, and Arnold surveyed his reflection. Yes, he thought. He was beautiful. He hoped it would be enough to save the Conclave. Doubt curled like a snake in his stomach, but he didn't know what else he could do.

Science Activity:

Fill a clear container halfway with water, then squeeze in some dish soap. Swish it around to make bubbles. Look at the bubbles in sunlight. (You might have to move your head around a bit to get the angle right, but can you see the pinpricks of color in each bubble? What colors do you see?

When light shining from overhead hits the surface of the bubble, some of it goes into the soap, but some of it reflects back. After the light goes through the soap, it hits the inside of the soap bubble, and again some of it reflects back.

These two reflections (one from the outside and one from the inside) combine to make colors. The different colors appear because the soap layer has different thicknesses in different places, changing how the light mixes.

The morning dawned bright and clear, and all the animals gathered for the coronation. Arnold hopped from foot to foot tasting the salty shells of the floor behind the stage. Nervously, he readjusted his outfit. The clear scales slid gently across one another, reflecting bright bands of iridescent blues, greens, reds, and ultra.

Where was the lion? He still hoped desperately to speak with him before the coronation.

A trio of French horns sounded, and the king appeared, sweeping right past Arnold without a second look and taking the podium.

The king looked out of breath as he scanned the crowd. He was saying something, but he was facing away from Arnold, and the crowd drowned out the lion's soft, commanding tone.

Time went too quickly, and suddenly the lion was gesturing to Arnold to take the stage.

Arnold took a deep breath to quell his shaking, and stepped out, hoping his beautiful colors would be enough.

✶

Out in the crowd, the snake was watching as the lion brought Arnold onto the stage. The snake's tongue flicked out and in, tasting the air. The heavy scent of the antelope overpowered almost everything else, but she caught a faint potato-like whiff of badger, and the strong, dusty smell of birds.

The antelope below her glowed warmly, and the crowd around her sent off waves of heat. Animals shifted and rustled, but she knew where they were by the heat they gave off, like warmth rising from sand.

The snake wished she was basking on warm sand now, not perched precariously on an antelope. Hopefully this ceremony would end soon. She could barely hear the lion over the stamping of paws. The vibrations ran up through the antelope, shaking its horns.

The Emperor Butterfly's New Clothes

> **Science Note:**
> Snakes have color vision too, but they are called 'dichromats,' meaning they see with two types of color receptors rather than the three that most humans have. Although they can only see in blues and greens, they have very good senses of smell. Some snakes can also sense heat, similar to the infrared of night-vision goggles! Additionally, they are very sensitive to vibrations, which they use to sense prey.

✽

Farther out, in the salty waters of the bay, the shark watched, too.

I should be queen, the shark thought, floating in her cold, salty domain. She squinted up at the hazy blue and green shapes. Each one sparked with electrical impulses, like flashes of lightning. Somewhere a quarter mile away a trickle of blood expanded in the ocean. She longed to seek it out. Overhead the great undulating heartbeat in the sky shifted and whirled, like some great prey object. Someday, she thought. Someday she would reach it, would catch and devour that giant in the sky. Perhaps then they would make her queen.

> **Science Note:**
>
> Sharks are probably color blind but can sense electric and magnetic fields! They use the earth's magnetic field to navigate (much like we use compasses). And they can sense the electrical impulses of heartbeats and nerves, which they use to sense their prey, even if their prey is hiding under sand!

Arnold stepped onto the stage, fluttering his wings and holding his antennae aloft. The marvelous suit shifted and articulated around him, like iridescent armor. He had never looked this incredible. This powerful.

He stepped purposefully over to join the lion who peered at him, looking surprised and perhaps . . . confused? Not the look of awe and respect Arnold had hoped for.

He glanced out at the crowd, his eyes flicking from the snake to the cold eyes of the shark, to Sheila's excited hopping form. Her eyes shone with pride, but the snake looked bored, the shark looked angry, and the birds looked mildly impressed at best.

> **Science Question:**
>
> Why do you think the snake and the shark might not be impressed? What do you think Arnold looks like to them?

The Emperor Butterfly's New Clothes

Arnold hopped and fluttered, flexing his wings faster and faster, turning this way and that. He caught the light and reflected it at all angles into the staring crowd.

"You can't beee serious," the bee said.

"He's so tiny," whispered the hippo.

"Clearly this is some kind of joke," the heron commented.

The bear threw up her paws. "I'm leaving. Anyone else coming?" She turned and began to lumber off, pushing her way through the crowd. Several animals began to stand and follow her.

The rest of the lion's speech could barely be heard as one by one, the animals began to get up and leave, looks of disgust on their faces.

Arnold barely heard anything as the lion finished his speech.

No one thought he was beautiful. If that had been what the lion had wanted, Arnold had failed.

✹

Late that evening, Arnold crouched on the same balcony where earlier he and Sheila had so hopefully constructed his new clothes. The moonlight pooled around him, revealing a world devoid of color.

Something flashed in the corner of his vision. A pair of widely spaced eyes reflecting the moonlight back to him. The figure approached, more shadow than shape, until he was so close he could have reached out and touched the flowing silver mane. It was the lion.

"I'm so sorry," Arnold said, hanging his head, his proboscis drooping. "I did my best to be as beautiful and as colorful as I could be. I am sorry that it wasn't enough. I'm sorry I caused the end of the Conclave."

The lion was silent for several seconds. "Is that what all that was? Oh my." He cleared his throat. "I do apologize, dear Arnold. It was lovely of you to put in so much effort, and I deeply regret that I left you . . . in the dark, as it were."

The lion glanced around. "I am told many animals have difficulty seeing in this time of day. Is that the case for you?"

Arnold frowned at the mighty king. "You can see in this?"

"Quite well, yes."

Arnold sighed. The king was so powerful he could even see in this terrible darkness.

Tears welled in his eyes, and his throat clenched. At last, he managed to get a few words out.

"Sir, if I may ask, why did you choose me for this role? What could I possibly help with?" He looked bitterly at the remains of his fabulous new clothes that Sheila had worked so hard on. "I did my best to be as beautiful as possible, but it wasn't enough."

"Oh, Arnold, I am so sorry." The lion removed his spectacles, polished them nervously with his mane, and replaced them. "It was not because you are beautiful that I chose you. Though, I have heard the birds say you are beautiful, and I am sure that is the case."

Arnold stared at the salty ground.

The lion cleared his throat. "My friend, I believe you misunderstand. You see, it is not your failing but mine. I can't even fully see what you are." The lion glanced around the moonlit balcony, staring thoughtfully up at the bright orb, its silvery light glinting off his mane. "I see the world in blues, greens, and yellows. The colors of my savannah home. Through many strange conversations I have come to suspect that there is much, much more to the world that I in fact cannot see at all." He glanced at Arnold. "For example, can you perhaps tell me how you managed to find your way to this remote island?"

Arnold frowned. "I followed the angle of the sky, of course."

"And . . . what is that?"

"The angle of the sky? It's the . . . the direction . . . that the sky points? I'm sorry, sir, I don't know how else to describe it."

"Did you know I asked the shark that as well, and she said there is a great heartbeat in the sky? Something akin to . . . nerve impulses and muscle twitches. Which apparently she can perceive. Remarkable."

The lion went on. "You might also be interested to know that I am unable to navigate long distances as you and the shark can. These features of the sky are . . . invisible to me."

Arnold didn't know what to say. There was something he could see that the great and mighty lion could not? It seemed quite unbelievable.

"This is why I made you king, Arnold. Not because you are beautiful, although you are. I believe that if the Conclave is to continue, we must better understand one another. We must see that in our incredible variety is great strength."

The lion looked down at his paws and was silent again. "My mother was a much stronger ruler than I have been," he said at last. Arnold shifted, confused. "She did something incredible, bringing us all together. None of us would have survived. I've . . . I've tried to live up to her, but I am afraid I haven't been up to the task."

Arnold could relate to being given a task that one did not feel well-suited for. He reached out a slender foreleg and gently patted a tuft of hair on the lion's tail. The lion didn't seem to notice.

The Emperor Butterfly's New Clothes

"There are as many ways of experiencing the world as there are ways of being, and it is time that someone with another perspective was king. I know it can be hard, or impossible, to understand each other, and to see how others see the world."

"Oh. I see," said Arnold, although he wasn't sure he did.

"I'm glad," the lion said. He tilted his head down, and in the moonlight, he suddenly looked very tired. "I'm sorry to pass this responsibility on to you, but I believe you will make a good king. Better than I have been, at any rate." He gave a long sigh. "To be honest, I am so glad to be able to do something else. Finally."

Arnold patted the lion's tuft of hair a little harder—but still reassuringly—but the lion didn't seem to notice.

Before Arnold could ask anything else, the lion had stalked off into the hazy darkness.

For a long time that night, Arnold sat in the dark, thinking about what the lion had said. Finally, he had an idea. And this time, he was certain it would work.

✦

"You want me to do hh-what?" Sheila asked.

Arnold repeated his idea.

"That—and my friend, I say this with all the respect in the world—sounds . . ."

"No, I know," Arnold said, "But . . . see the thing is, the reason the clothes didn't work is that different animals see differently."

One of the badgers cleared its throat, looked for a moment like it was going to say something, and then stopped.

"But . . . color is color, isn't it?" Sheila asked.

"I thought so, too, but then I talked to the lion." Arnold explained about how the snake saw heat and felt vibrations, and the shark sensed electric fields.

"But surely they can see ultra?" Sheila said. "And taste the ground with their feet!"

"Apparently not!" Arnold said.

Sheila looked horrified at the thought. "A world without being able to see ultra . . ."

"So, you can see we need a new strategy. They couldn't even see my clothes!"

Sheila's eyes lit up. "Aaah! Yes! That makes perfect sense. No one wouldn't like my clothes. I knew there had to be some explanation."

One of the badgers raised a finger and opened her mouth, then shut it again, shaking her head.

"So, we just need to make something—"

"—That they can all see!" Sheila hopped from side to side, then held up her foreleg. Arnold stared at her, confused, until she grasped his leg and high-fived it. Then he grinned, nodding, and they high-fived again.

The badger finally interjected. "Are you *completely sure* that the solution is clothes, your highness?"

Arnold nodded firmly. Yes. He was sure. This was going to work.

The Emperor Butterfly's New Clothes

They had just put the finishing touches on Arnold's fantastic new clothes when a loud uproar came from the direction of the cathedral. Arnold looked immediately at the security badgers.

A young badger rushed in and whispered in one of their ears, shoving something into their hand then glanced wide-eyed at Arnold.

This badger now approached Arnold, holding out what appeared to be a note. She cleared her throat. "'Scuse me, your . . . highness. Sorry to interrupt. The lion left this note."

Arnold scanned the noble cursive writing. It was a formal resignation, and it indicated that the lion had left to return to his home on the savannah.

A tremor went through him. The lion had left? Just left him to run things?

"Sir, we don't know how, but word's already gotten out. The snake seems to be making a speech. You'd better go."

Arnold threw on his new clothes and fluttered as fast as he could to the cathedral.

The snake, the bear, and the heron all stood on the podium, the other animals watching.

"We need an actual strong leader," the bear shouted, clenching her paws and brandishing her fists.

"On the contrary, we need an intelligent leader," the heron said, looking down her beak at the others.

"Thissss is ssstupid," the snake snapped. "We don't need Conclavessss anymore. Let'ssss go."

Arnold stood in the wings, wondering if the Conclave was about to end.

Maybe the bear or the heron would hold it together. Maybe the bear or the heron would be a better leader than he would, too. Behind him, though, he saw Sheila, her eyes wide. There were so many other tiny creatures like her and like Arnold. Maybe the lion was right that they needed to be seen. He stamped his feet a few times, taking one last taste of the salty floor. Then, he switched on his suit and strode out onto the stage.

Little sparks of static—from a particularly staticky fabric that Sheila usually avoided—flashed up and down as he walked. The shark and a few other animals immediately glanced his way, their mouths hanging open.

Warm rocks that had heated in the sun and then been made into thick, hot scales, clattered and clanked, dangling from Arnold's body. The snake turned her head and stared in confusion, her tongue flicking in and out. Arnold squished some of the little bulbs Sheila had attached to his vest, releasing clouds of strange and interesting scents that silenced the nearby animals.

Arnold danced purposefully, sending out flashes of heat, scent, and electricity. The whole crowd went utterly silent. A rush of pride went through him. They'd done it. These clothes could be seen by all the animals!

The bear gave a furious roar. "Enough distractions! I declare myself the new king!" She lunged for Arnold, swatting at him with an enormous, heavy paw.

Arnold's vision was highly attuned to movement, though, and he saw her coming as if in slow motion. He had plenty of time to react, to think what to do, and he easily dodged out of the way.

Next came the snake, though, with her quick tongue, shooting towards him.

The clothes were a bright beacon, leading her straight to him.

But clothes could be used to hide, just as easily, Arnold realized as she streaked towards him. He dodged to the side again, pulling a scaly cloak around himself as he did so. The cloak blocked all the heat and scent from escaping—Sheila had been very excited about the idea of a dramatic reveal as he pulled the cloak back, but now Arnold used the dramatic reveal in reverse, quickly hiding himself.

The snake whizzed right past Arnold, and a zap of electricity arced from his clothes to her as she went by.

"Ouch!" she hissed, weaving her head this way and that, looking for the now-invisible Arnold.

Sheila fist-pumped the air and hopped back and forth.

The heron's sharp beak stabbed towards Arnold, but he fluttered out of the way, pulling an emergency cord Sheila had installed. Another layer of metallic, reflective scales unrolled, flashing in the heron's eyes. She closed them briefly against the glare, and then Arnold moved to the back of the stage, readjusting his suit into camouflage mode. The clear scales aligned in such a way to match the color of the wall behind him, and in an instant, Arnold disappeared.

The heron, the snake, and the bear looked around one another in confusion. None of them were able to sense him.

Out in the bay, the shark began to laugh.

She glided forward, the water animals giving her a wide berth.

"Impressive, little butterfly," she said. "How did you do it? How do you make such large heartbeats?"

She waited, but Arnold didn't move. None of them could see him now, and he wasn't going to risk changing that.

He didn't want to be king, he just wanted to run. But his eyes again found Sheila. She looked so proud, so happy. He couldn't let her down.

If he revealed himself, the animals might eat him right away. But he couldn't run. They would find him eventually.

He thought of the lion. What would the lion do in this situation? But the lion hadn't wanted this responsibility either. It was too much. Was anyone strong enough to hold the Conclave together?

Another idea hit him. This time, surprisingly, it didn't even have to do with clothes.

He let off a huge shower of sparks and flashes, the largest wave of heat and smell that the suit could produce, and he leapt back into the center of the stage, so close to the bear's heavy paws, the heron's sharp beak, and the snake's venomous fangs.

They were momentarily stunned into silence, and into this silence Arnold spoke as loudly as he could.

"There shouldn't be a king anymore," he shouted. "But the Conclave should continue. We all have such different ways of seeing the world, and such different skills. We need to work together. For my first and only act as king, before I resign, I hereby appoint the heron, the bear, the snake, and . . ." he paused but, no, it was important to include everyone, "the shark, along with Sheila the jumping spider, to be on a special Conclave Council. That way, all of you will run the Conclave together."

A wide, toothy grin split the shark's face. The bear sat back on her heels, her paws thumping down onto her legs. The snake's tongue flicked thoughtfully in and out.

The heron rearranged her wings on her shoulders and was the first to break the surprised silence. "I believe this is very wise," she said. "We are stronger together, and we see the world more clearly together. Each of seeing our own different parts of it."

The bear scratched her head, but she slowly nodded along.

The snake rolled her eyes and glanced at the door. "Fine . . . I ssssuppossse."

A malevolent light flashed in the shark's eyes. She was clearly plotting her overthrow of the council already, but no one seemed to mind.

Sheila hopped back and forth, bouncing from animal to animal as she zig-zagged up to the stage. "Fantastic! Absolutely fan-tastic, everyone. This is going to be great. So great." She sized up the bear. "A cloak. Yes—no. Matching cloaks! For everyone! Very regal, I think, yes? No?"

"Can mine do the zappy thing?" the snake asked.

"Of course, yes!" Sheila said.

"You can leave the smells off mine," the heron sniffed.

"Oh, no. You're sure? Okaaay . . ."

The shark did try to take over several times, in increasingly creative and malevolent ways. But they managed to thwart her attempts.

From then on, the animal council ruled wisely and effectively, slowly learning more and more about how they each perceived the world.

As for Arnold, he was mostly glad to no longer have the responsibility of being king. He fluttered off to find those food bushes that had smelled so good. They tasted just as wonderful as they'd smelled. The lion was never seen or heard from again, except that every few months Arnold would get a small gift in the mail. He didn't know for sure, but he suspected these were thank you and apology gifts from the lion, for leaving him to deal with the Conclave alone.

Sheila, despite her rigorous duties on the council, still took time to make many beautiful, colorful sets of clothing for many different animals, and using all the different animal senses. And she and Arnold remained lifelong friends.

Science Writing Prompt:

Pick an animal and research its senses. What colors can it see? What is its sense of smell like? How does it hear or taste? What kinds of details of its environment is it likely to notice? Now try writing a scene or short story where it uses its senses to solve a problem.

Some interesting animals to pick would be the platypus, the star-nosed mole, the hammerhead shark, the mantis shrimp, cavefish, dolphins, or bats.

See What Arnold Sees: Polarized Light

We human beings have very good vision! We can see a wide range of colors, and a lot of detail even at long distances (not as much as hawks can, but still a lot more than many animals!) But there's a lot we can't see.

One of these things we can't see is what's called the 'polarization' of light.

Have you ever played with a jump rope? Can you imagine having your friend hold one end of the jump rope, and you hold the other end, and shake it up and down?

You can see what waves on strings are like using this simulation from the University of Colorado:

Some things to try with the simulation:

1. Set the damping to zero. (Damping is just the way that friction slows waves down eventually.
2. Keep one end fixed, then grab the wrench and move it up and down and watch what happens on the string.
3. You could also try setting the end to "oscillate" which means to move up and down or back and forth in a regular way (going the same speed back and forth.)

It turns out that, in some ways, light rays act like a wave travelling along a string.

Now, imagine that instead of shaking your jump rope up and down, you wiggle it from side to side. The wave would now be wiggling like a snake horizontally, instead of vertically like rolling hills. This is something light can do, too! In fact, light could be wiggling at any angle. The tilt of that light is called its "polarization"

Most light is a mix of rays tilted at different angles, but some light, especially light that has reflected off of water, is all tilted at the same angle. We call this 'polarized light'.

Butterflies can see the polarization of light! It's hard to imagine what this might look like to Arnold. Who knows what it would be like to see the angle the light rays are wiggling at?

It might be like a slightly different flavor of each color. So, Arnold could look at blue light and he might see just regular unpolarized blue, or he might look at the sky and see that it was polarized in a certain direction. It would still look blue, but he'd know which direction it was tilted in.

The Emperor Butterfly's New Clothes

Even though we can't see polarized light ourselves, there is a way for you to get a sense of what this looks like for Arnold! Scientists have invented filters that only let light through that's polarized in a certain direction.

You might even have one of these around your home! Have you been to a 3-D movie recently? Those glasses you wear are filters for polarized light! One of the lenses is tilted at one angle, and the other is at a different angle.

3-D movies work by showing you two full movies at once. One of the movies is made of light polarized in one direction, which is able to get through your glasses to your left eye, and the other movie is made with light polarized at a different angle which is able to get through your glasses to your right eye! By showing each of our eyes a different movie, the filmmakers can make us feel like we're looking at something 3-dimensional!

If you don't have any 3-D glasses, do you have any sunglasses that are supposed to reduce glare?

Most light is unpolarized, but it turns out that when light reflects off water or metal, it becomes polarized. (Think of the sparkly, bright way that light reflecting off water looks. That's horizontally polarized light!) Some sunglasses have a filter that very cleverly only lets vertically polarized light through. That way, you don't get that super bright reflected light hurting your eyes.

The third option is that you can buy light polarizing filters on the internet. I bought these: Polarized Film Sheets 3 PCS 7.8 x11.8inches/20x30cm Polarizer Linear Polarizing Filter Non-Adhesive for Educational Physics Photography Lighting.

They have a protective coating on both sides that you have to peel off, but once you do, you have a very nice tool for seeing how the world looks to a butterfly!

Once you have 3-D glasses, glare-reducing sunglasses, or a polarizing sheet, head outside. If you can, try to find someplace where there are reflections you can look at, like bright light reflecting off a car or a pool of water. Hold the sheet out in front of you, looking at the world through the sheet. Now rotate the sheet slowly and watch how the world changes. At a certain angle, you'll see the bright lights disappear. Anything that disappears at a certain angle is polarized light.

You can look at the sky through your filter, too. Rotate the filter, and you'll notice the sky gets darker and brighter. This is because the light from the sun gets slightly polarized as it scatters in our upper atmosphere.

Further Reading

There is a Pulitzer Prize winning book called Immense World that goes into incredible, fascinating detail about the senses of different animals, and the different worlds they live in as a result. I highly recommend it!

The Wayfarer's Scepter

Written by Sarah Allen

Illustrated by Marie Delwart

Formatted by Sue Balcer

Once upon a time, on a small planet about the size of our moon, there lived a brave adventurer. Unfortunately, she had no time for adventures.

Zara was the Wayfarer, keeper of the scepter, and last in a long line of those who could traverse the dangerous, ever shifting, dragon-filled lands at the equator and carry messages between the small kingdoms of the north and south poles.

The scepter was cold iron in her hand as she left the gates of the south pole, beginning yet again the trek through the wastelands to the north. Behind her, the southern lights bloomed and shifted in the sky, like flows of glowing algae.

Sarah Allen

In the cold pinpricks of the stars behind them, Zara could feel the eyes of her mother, and her grandmother, and her great grandmother before that. Each of them had spent their lives moving first north and then south, pinging between the two nations, carrying gifts and threats between them.

The Wayfairer's Scepter

Zara bounded off a cliff, sailing through the air and drifting slowly towards the rocky ground below. Gravity on Zara's planet was much less than that on ours. Her wool cloak billowed around her. She wore a silver circlet in her black hair, so that she would be recognized as the Wayfarer wherever she went.

At the bottom, she crouched behind a boulder as a dragon roared past in a gust of heat and teeth. It was better not to be seen than to have to fight, Zara had learned.

A red silk cord was looped around her wrist, the other end affixed to the center of her staff. When the dragon had passed, she lifted the cord, suspending the staff from its middle. Idly, she watched it twist and turn, until at last it settled, pointing due north.

> ### Science Note:
> Zara's scepter is an iron magnet. This means that it will try to line up with whatever magnetic fields are around. Zara's planet, just like ours, has a giant magnetic field surrounding it. And her scepter, just like our compasses, lines up with that field.

No one knew how the scepter worked. It was the only tool they had for navigating the planet's surface, and she had the only one.

She set off, determined to cover at least a hundred miles that day. With bounding leaps, she flew across the ground, soaring from one rocky outcrop to the next. The ground beneath her shook with constant earthquakes. The land between the two kingdoms was always rearranging itself, another reason the journey between them was so hazardous. No maps could be made. And the stars themselves shifted as the planet tumbled in an irregular orbit.

Despite the vast distances she covered, the journey would take her several months. Several months of hiding from dragons, of watching for lava flows, of wishing she had someone to talk to besides the stars.

In her long run over the next few days, her thoughts turned to the notes in the leather satchel she carried. She remembered her mother describing the gifts she'd carried between the two kingdoms, but in Zara's lifetime it had only been letters. She wasn't supposed to read them, but she did.

They grew angrier and angrier, filled with recrimination. It seemed to Zara they only wanted someone to blame for every problem. The letters grew more and more scathing every year.

One night, as Zara lay tucked between two boulders, feeling the heat rising from the stones below her, watching the stars flickering overhead and hearing the distant roars and glimmers of dragon fire on the horizon, her thoughts turned again to that secret dream of hers. The one the stars could never know about.

She wanted to explore. Every year she traversed the planet, straight from pole to pole, as quickly as she could, carrying those messages. But sometimes in the wastelands she saw things. Strange rock formations. Caves. What looked like ancient paths. Sometimes she even thought her scepter wanted her to go somewhere other than where her duty called her. Its rough iron point tilted slightly, or dipped, as if something wavered, or something other than the poles was drawing her.

The Wayfairer's Scepter

> **Science Note:**
>
> If you've ever used compasses, you might have noticed that magnets can interfere with their readings. That's because a compass lines up with whatever magnetic field is strongest. Usually, that's the Earth's magnetic field, but if there's a magnet or a big deposit of magnetized iron nearby, it'll line up with that.

But Zara did her duty. She did her duty as her mother had, as her grandmother had, and she sailed across the land, running as fast as she could, carrying the messages that grew more and more hateful.

Months passed, and the northern aurora bloomed before her in the night sky. A few weeks later, she arrived finally at the great silver gates of the northern kingdom.

> **Science Note:**
>
> Have you ever seen the Northern Lights, also called the Aurora Borealis? What we see is our planet's magnetic field protecting us from radiation and charged particles emitted by the sun. Storms on the surface of the sun send out clouds of charged particles in the solar winds. These hit our planet and are deflected by the magnetic field. These particles interact with our upper atmosphere, causing it to glow.

She found a great crowd awaiting her, the Festival of the Wayfarer, with thousands gathered to hear the news she brought from the southern kingdom.

As always, Zara cringed from the noise, the press of crowds, the vast surging energy of so many people. But this time, there was a feverish quality, a rage. People shouted strange questions at her, like whether anyone from the southern kingdom had tried to steal her scepter from her. Zara pulled away, afraid that if she answered their questions truthfully, they would think she'd sided with the other kingdom. It was better not to be seen than have to fight, Zara thought again to herself.

The guards escorted her straight to the High Council of the North.

Here, the nine heads of state loomed down at her from a glittering table. She stood in the center of the hall to give her report and pass along the letters.

What am I doing? she thought, watching their faces redden with anger as they read the messages.

She stood silently as they discussed above her what threats, which insults, they might send. But something shifted, something inside her turned to iron as hard as her scepter as she listened. *I won't pass on their messages,* she thought. *But they'll think I've sided with the others,* came her next thought, and the iron went frosty. What would they do to her?

She saw their faces as dragons, spewing hateful breath, and wished she were alone staring up at the sky.

They began collecting their messages.

I won't, she thought. *I don't want to contribute to so much hate.* But what if they took her scepter?

They paused to argue over the wording of their insults.

I won't, she thought more firmly. But what if they used the scepter themselves? They could do real damage to the other kingdom that way.

"Do you have the gift?" one of the council members asked another.

Zara was brought back to the present. They had a gift for the other kingdom? Maybe despite everything, there was hope.

"Yes," the other said solemnly. She lifted a sealed package. "This carries the sickness."

Zara's stomach swirled, she felt lightheaded. She had to speak up.

"You're going to hurt them?" she asked.

"They have been a threat to us long enough," said one.

"We have to defend ourselves," said another.

"It's only a matter of time before they do the same," said a third.

"No," said Zara. The single word rang through the hall, silence descending in its wake.

All nine members of the council stared at her.

"I won't send a weapon, from either of you," Zara said.

"She's joined them," a council member whispered.

The others looked down at the messages she'd brought, backing away from them and wiping their hands.

"What weapon did they send?" another member asked.

"They didn't send any weapon!" Zara shouted. "They're just like you! Afraid and angry at your insults!"

"They started it. We are defending ourselves."

"No one knows who started it," Zara said, her voice ringing out, loud and sure now. "But you're both perpetuating it. And I won't help you any longer."

She turned to go. "I will be back next year. If you have something nice to say, I will carry your messages then."

But the doors slammed shut before she could take a step. At a gesture from the council, the guards closed in around her.

Zara looked down at the red silk encircling her wrist. They would take the scepter. They would send their weapons to the south. Both kingdoms would be destroyed in the ensuing war.

Something roared up inside her, hotter than dragon flame, like starlight, like burning suns, like a shifting aurora sparkling across the sky. She gripped her scepter, raised it over her head, and smashed it onto the floor.

The scepter was iron. She had used it to battle dragons, to pry boulders off their perches. It was incredibly strong, but some other force filled her, and the scepter shattered into a thousand tiny fragments.

The sharp bits of iron scattered across the floor, the guards and council members cringing backwards. Strangely, they all aligned, pointing away from Zara like sharp little flower petals.

The Wayfairer's Scepter

> **Science Activity:**
> If you have some magnets (maybe some small ones on your fridge) try bringing them close to one another. If you spin one, what happens to the other one?

The guards withdrew from Zara, no one was brave enough to approach the girl who had just shattered an iron bar.

She swept the shards into her cloak and left, flying over the heads of the crowds and fleeing the city.

"What have I done?" she thought that night, sitting alone again with the shards of the staff her mother had entrusted to her.

She cried, letting the shards run through her fingers. But then she noticed something. Each little fragment aligned with the next. They all pointed from south to north, just like her scepter had. In fact, each one was like a tiny scepter itself.

It hit her like a burst of dragon fire. "I don't have to be the only one anymore."

She scrubbed the tears from her cheeks, took off her circlet, and made her way back to the town. Hiding her identity, she began to spend time with people. She spoke to innkeepers, to dressmakers, to schoolteachers and bakers. She found that most people were not as angry as they'd seemed, and to those who seemed kind, and seemed inclined to explore, she gave a fragment of her scepter.

Over the next few years, she travelled back and forth between the kingdoms, finding kind and brave adventurers to gift the iron shards to. Slowly, these people began to traverse the planet themselves.

As more and more people traveled between the two kingdoms, met one another, and talked, the anger and distrust dissipated. Soon there was trade and friendship between the two nations.

For a while, Zara helped them traverse the planet, but soon she set off on her own explorations. She found, with her own tiny shard, that there were more deposits of iron throughout the world, and that many of them had this same magnetic property. If she found iron that didn't have this property, she found that her own shard could change the iron so that it worked the way the scepter had. Soon everyone was able to traverse the planet, flying and taming dragons and discovering new lands, guided by the magnetic field of the planet, to which her little iron magnets aligned.

And as for Zara, she no longer had to traverse the wastes alone, hiding from dragons and keeping silent, ricocheting between enemies. She explored the world, making many friends and seeing many wonders. And everyone lived happily ever after.

What is Zara's Scepter?

Zara's scepter is a magnet. There are lots of types of magnets, but hers is made of iron, as are fridge magnets.

Magnets can be made of many types of materials, because all atoms have little magnetic fields around them. Iron works really well, though, because all those little fields can be lined up in the same direction. They add together and make a bigger, powerful magnet. We call this "being magnetized".

You might have noticed that sometimes when spoons come out of the dishwasher they slightly stick to each other. Sometimes the dishwasher magnetizes the metal of the silverware.

What is a magnetic field? Well, it's the space around a magnet where any charge moving through that space will be affected by the magnet. See, magnetic fields are created by moving charges, and they affect moving charges, causing them to turn.

In a way, magnets have teeny tiny little moving charges in them that create these fields.

We can also create magnetic fields with electric current, which is just a bunch of charges flowing along together. If you have a loop of wire and you send some electricity through it, you'll have a magnetic field that looks exactly like one from a magnet.

One thing that makes magnets so incredibly useful is that they always want to line up with one another. If you have two magnets next to each other, they'll spin so that they're facing the same way (if they're able to.)

So how does Zara use her scepter to navigate? Well, her planet, just like our planet, has a magnetic field around it. Her scepter, being a magnet, always wants to align itself with the magnetic field. So, she can hold up her scepter, dangling from the cord, and it will spin until it lines up with the field. Then she'll know which way North is!

Our magnetic field around the Earth actually goes from the south pole to the north pole, but it sometimes switches!

It wanders around a little, moving a few degrees here and there every year (we call this the Magnetic Declination) and sometimes switches sides completely. The last time it switched was around 780,000 years ago!

Some animals like sea turtles and salmon can sense the magnetic field of the earth and use it to navigate, too.

What happens if you break a bar magnet in half? You might think that you'd have a little north pole and a little south pole, but actually what you get is two smaller magnets, each with their own north and south poles. This is why in the story, when Zara breaks her scepter, all the tiny shards still function as tiny scepters.

Magnets Can Generate Electricity

Magnets can push electric charges around, which is incredibly useful because we can use this fact to create electricity!

This is something called Faraday's Law. The University of Colorado has a great PhET Simulation you can play around with. Either follow the link below or search for "Phet Faraday's Law"

To play with the simulation, click and hold on the magnet to drag it around. Bring it closer and farther from the coil of wires. What do you notice? Does the light bulb light up when the magnet is moving? When it is stopped? How can you make the bulb as bright as possible?

This is one of the main ways we generate renewable energy! Hydroelectric dams and wind turbines both work this way.

In hydroelectric dams, water flow turns turbines connected to a generator, which usually has a rotor with magnets spinning inside coils of wire. This movement induces an electric current in the wire.

Wind turbines work similarly, with the wind turning the blades connected to a rotor that spins magnets near coils of wire in the generator, producing electricity.

If you'd like to try to build one on your own, the Exploratorium has some good instructions for making a simple generator that lights a bulb:

Make a Generator

Make Your Own Scepter (Compass)

Materials

Piece of Foam
Needle
Magnet
Glass of Water
Sense of Adventure

Instructions

1. Slide magnet across the needle several times to magnetism it (like you're sharpening a knife, only go one way and not back and forth.)
2. Spear the needle through the piece of foam.
3. Place the needle in the water. It should float on top. (The foam is like a little floaty for the needle.)
4. The needle should now point North-South, like a compass.
5. Try bringing the magnet near the glass and watch how the needle moves.
6. If it doesn't work, try magnetizing the needle again.

Thanks for Reading!

Thanks so much for reading, I hope you enjoyed the book! If you have a moment, I would greatly appreciate an honest review on Amazon.

If you'd like more physics stories, worksheets, and games, you can check out my website: www.MathwithSarah.com.

You can also sign up for the Sometimes Science newsletter, where I sporadically send out updates about what I'm working on, free resources for learning physics in fun, hands-on ways (preferably in stories), and the occasional meteor shower heads-up.

About the Author

Sarah Allen was a math and physics tutor for twenty years before becoming a full-time fantasy writer. She earned her undergraduate degree in physics with both college and departmental honors at the University of Washington, and a master's degree in Cognition and Learning from Columbia University.

Her all-time favorite book is *The Phantom Tollbooth*, and her current goal in life, besides growing a few flowers that are not eaten by deer, is to write the sorts of physics books she would have wanted as a kid.

Printed in Great Britain
by Amazon